Cassie's Crutches

Story by Cameron Macintosh

Illustrations by Nathalie Ortega

Contents

Chapter 1

A Fall at Basketball

On Saturday, Cassie was playing basketball with some friends.

"Catch, Cassie!" shouted Jade.

Cassie jumped up to catch the ball.

Then, she ran to the basket with the ball.
But she slipped on a stone and fell over.

"Dad, I have hurt my ankle!" she cried.

Dad ran over to Cassie.

"Your ankle does not look good," he said.
"I'll have to take you to the hospital."

Chapter 2

At the Hospital

At the hospital, Doctor Patel looked at Cassie's ankle.

"You have twisted your ankle," she said. "You will need to wear one of these."

Doctor Patel held up a bandage.

"I'm scared that it will hurt," said Cassie.

"I'll be very careful when I put it on," said Doctor Patel. "I won't hurt you."

"Here are some crutches, too,"
said Doctor Patel.
"You will need these to help you walk."

Cassie walked around the room slowly. Dad and Doctor Patel walked beside her.

"I'm not very good at this," said Cassie.

"You are doing very well, Cassie," said Doctor Patel.

Chapter 3

Back to School

On Wednesday, Cassie went back to school.
She needed Dad's help to get into the car.

"I don't want to go to school," she said to Dad.
"It will be too hard to move around with these crutches."

"You will be okay at school," said Dad.
"Your teacher, Ms Tran, and your friends will help you."

At school, Cassie walked slowly
with her crutches.

She went into the classroom with Dad.

Ms Tran came over.
"I'm very happy to see you, Cassie," she said.
"Let me help you with your things."

"Come and sit down," said Jack, pulling out Cassie's chair.

"Here is a chair for your foot!" said Kira.

At play time, Cassie walked to the chair under the tree with Jack and Kira.

"You are very good at walking with your crutches!" said Kira.

"Yes," said Jack.
"You are good at going up and down the steps, too."

"Thank you," said Cassie, smiling. "Maybe it's not so bad having crutches after all!"